D0988175

Published in Great Britain in 2002 by Hodder Wayland,
an imprint of Hodder Children's Books

This edition re-issued in 2008 by Wayland

Britain Library Cataloguing in Publication Date
Bradman, Tony, 1954-
Litter Flame and the Great Queen : the story of Boudicca.
- (Historial storybooks )
1.Boudicca, Queen, consort of Prasutagus, King of the Iceni, d. 60
2.Queen - Great Britain - Juvenile fiction 3.Great Britain -
History - Roman period, 55B.C.-449A.D. - Juvenile fiction
4.Historial fiction 5.Children's stories
I.Title II.Moulder, Bob
823.9'14[J]

ISBN 978 0 7502 5430 4

Printed in China

Wayland
338 Euston Road,
London NW1 3BH

Wayland is a division of hachette Children's Books,
an Hachette Livre UK Company

www.hachettelivre.co.uk

# The Story of
# Boudicca

*Tony Bradman*

Illustrated by Bob Moulder

WAYLAND

# Boudicca

**55-54 BC** Julius Caesar made two military expeditions to Britain, but withdrew without making the island part of the Roman Empire.

**AD 43** The Emperor Claudius invaded Britain with a large army. The southern tribes were defeated. Some, like the Iceni, became Roman allies.

**AD 43-58** The Romans continued their conquest of Britain, moving west and north.

**AD 59?** Prasutagus, king of the Iceni, died. The Romans demanded that the Iceni's territory be incorporated into the empire. Boudicca, queen of the Iceni, was insulted.

**AD 60** Suetonius Paulinus, governor of Roman Britain, campaigned in Wales against the Celtic priests (the druids) on the island of Anglesey.

**AD 60** The Iceni rose in revolt against the Romans. Colchester, London and St Albans were destroyed. Suetonius Paulinus returned from Wales to crush the revolt in a great battle, probably somewhere in the Midlands. Boudicca died, almost certainly by suicide.

**AD 61-71** The Romans punished the rebels harshly, and Britain began its transformation into a province of the Roman Empire.

No one knows the exact dates of Boudicca's birth, marriage or death.

If you'd like to read more about Boudicca, try Richard Brassey's book *Brilliant Brits: Boudica* (published by Orion Children's Books, 2006).

# Chapter 1
# The Shadow of War

*Autumn,* AD 59.

My name is Tara, I am twelve summers old, and I am proud to be a daughter of the Iceni. In our tongue that means 'The Tribe of the Horse People', and we have lived in the land the Romans call Britain since before remembering.

We breed our fine horses and cattle and sheep, and we hunt in the forests and fish in the streams. We sow our crops of wheat and corn and barley and harvest them when the time comes. We worship our gods, Epona the Horse Lord, Cernunnos the Horned God, Morrigan the Three-in-One Goddess.

Such is the life I have always known, a happy life… Or, at least, it should be. But there is a sadness in my family. I am my parents' only living child – my mother gave birth to three babies after me, all of them dying quickly.

Another is due to be born in the spring, a hope and a worry together.

A shadow has fallen over the Iceni too, a
shadow I can see in the eyes of the elders in
our village, in my mother's eyes as well.
The shadow of war.

And it is all the fault of the Romans and
their greed for land and gold.

Twice the Romans have come to Britain.
Over a hundred summers ago, Julius Caesar
brought an army in ships. He fought great
battles with the tribes to the south of us,
then returned across the narrow sea. And
four summers before I was born, the
Emperor Claudius sent another army – this
time to conquer.

The southern tribes went on the warpath
again, and were defeated. But the Iceni
took a different way, hoping that the
storms of war would pass us by…

'I don't understand,' I said to my father
today. 'I thought our king had a treaty with
the Romans. Doesn't that mean they
should leave us alone?'

'But King Prasutagus has died, Little Flame,' said my father, his voice fierce, using the nickname he gave me because of my red hair and my fiery temper. 'And the Romans say that now we must be part of their empire.'

The king's body was barely cold before Roman soldiers and tax collectors swooped to strip his lands of everything. Worse, they flogged Queen Boudicca and attacked both her daughters. It was a terrible insult, and the whole tribe is hungry for vengeance.

But Rome is a powerful enemy. I have seen the soldiers marching down the trackway past our village, the crests on their helmets nodding, their eagle standards tall and proud, their steel-shod sandals thumping like the drum-beats of our warrior dances, but harder, and somehow relentless…

Tonight our village priest Dragorix called a council. The men's eyes gleamed in the firelight with thoughts of war.

Dragorix spoke of sacrifices too, the kind that were made in the old days – a human life given to the gods so they would give us victory.

Tonight only a lamb was sacrificed. But my blood still ran cold at the sight of Dragorix raising his knife over its small body... I glanced at my mother and father, and thought I would give anything to keep us all safe.

But what can one Little Flame do against the great storm brewing?

# Chapter 2
# The Coming of Boudicca

*Spring,* AD *60.*

The winter passed, and the men of our village made ready for war. My father sharpened his sword and dagger and spears, and polished his long shield till it shone.

The Romans, of course, knew nothing. We kept our preparations secret from the soldiers and tax collectors who came to the village and treated us like slaves. But we know everything we need to know about the Romans.

We know that the biggest part of the Roman army is in the west with the governor, Suetonius Paulinus. News has come that he has attacked Mona, the Sacred Island, and massacred the priests who live there to break their power forever. Dragorix wailed when he heard that.

Now the queen has sent a summons to each village, and the gathering of the Fighting Host has begun. It seems that every day yet another war band passes our village, making for the Hosting Place, a day's ride distant.

My mother gave birth three days ago, and all went well. The baby is a boy, and he seems strong. My parents have named him Bryn, and I love to hold him in my arms, stare into his deep blue eyes and kiss his soft skin…

Then we heard that the queen herself was heading our way. She arrived this evening, as the sun was setting, and the whole village came out to see her. She rode in a chariot drawn by two fine horses, her daughters beside her, the warriors of her bodyguard following on their prancing war ponies.

Boudicca is tall, and has long red hair, the same colour as mine. She wears a thick gold torc round her neck, and a cloak fastened with a gold brooch.

The queen decided to stay the night here, which is a great honour for our village. Everyone gathered in the hall of our chieftain to watch her feast. The warriors of her bodyguard stood behind her, the firelight playing on their scars, their tattoos, their war paint, the heron feathers in their spiked hair.

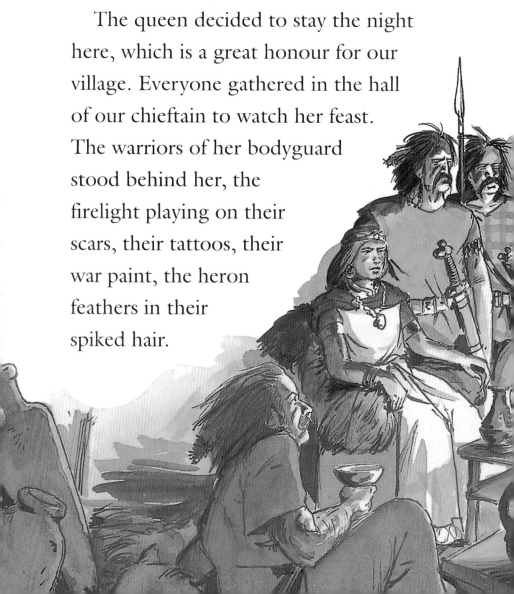

'Come, priest,' said Boudicca at last, calling Dragorix forward. 'Prophesy for me what is to be. Will I drive the Romans from our ancient lands?'

'I see fire and much blood,' Dragorix groaned. 'But Adraste, goddess of war, has need of a sacrifice from us, a sacrifice such as in the old days…'

I was at the back of the hall with my
mother and father and the baby, and just
then, Bryn started to cry, his tiny voice
suddenly loud in the quiet.

Dragorix whirled round, his crazed eyes
blazing, and pointed at us.

'It is a sign from Adraste!' he cried.
'The baby will be our sacrifice!'

The queen nodded, and the tallest of her warriors strode towards us. My mother screamed, and something snapped inside me. I pulled the dagger from my father's belt and stepped between the warrior and my family.

'NO!' I shouted, holding the dagger up. The warrior paused, and looked round at the queen. 'Take me instead,' I said. 'I will be the sacrifice…'

'Tara!' my mother cried out. 'Little Flame!' moaned my father.

'Seize her!' Dragorix yelled, and more warriors moved forward.

'Stop!' said Queen Boudicca, and the
hall fell silent. Then she came over and
smiled. 'Tell me, child,' she said. 'Would
you threaten your queen with that dagger
if I tried to take your brother and do as
the priest demands?'

'I would,' I said. I swallowed hard, but
I meant it, I really did.

'Well, then… Little Flame,' she said, glancing at her daughters. 'You and I share more than just the colour of our hair.' Then she turned and raised her voice. 'Let there be no sacrifice here tonight, of this baby boy or his sister. And let no man harm this child or her family, whatever the future holds…'

Boudicca left the next morning, with her tattooed warriors and Dragorix and the fighting men of the village. My father went too, riding his horse.

Mother and I stood on the trackway till we could see him no more.

# Chapter 3
# Battles Won – and Lost

*Summer,* AD *60.*

News came fast after that. Other tribes rose against the Romans and joined Queen Boudicca – our old enemies the Catuvellauni from the west, the Parisi from the north, the Trinovantes from the south.

Now the Romans realized they were in danger, but it was too late. The tribes fell on their new city of Camulodunum and besieged it. Two days later it was burned to the ground, and every man, woman and child in it slaughtered.

Such was the terrible vengeance of Boudicca, great Queen of the Iceni.

We heard that a Roman legion had set out from its fort at Lindum in the north to put down the rising. But Boudicca laid an ambush for the Romans, wiped out half the legionaries, and sent the rest scurrying back to their fort.

And then Boudicca destroyed two more Roman cities, Londinium and Verulamium, and massacred their inhabitants as well. Suetonius Paulinus was marching from the west with as many soldiers as he could muster…

But Boudicca's host outnumbered the Romans ten to one, so most of the people in the village thought that Boudicca was bound to win.

I wasn't so sure, and wondered how my father was, if he was still alive.

Then, a week ago, came the terrible news that Boudicca was defeated, that the revolt had been crushed! A messenger rode through the village on a fast pony, spreading the word, but didn't stop to answer any of our questions.

So it was only yesterday that we found out just what had happened.

Late in the evening a small band of men trailed into the village, most of them wounded, half of them walking, their horses having been killed. And there was my father, being helped along by two other men, one leg dragging.

We quickly got him into our house and saw that he was shivering, so we covered him with furs. Mother fed him some warm broth, then looked at the wound on his leg while I took care of Bryn.

'The Romans were waiting for us, Little Flame,' Father whispered at last. 'They were drawn up in three lines at the end of a narrow valley, with thick woods beyond it. Our chariots charged once, twice, and almost broke their shield wall. We charged again, but then somehow everything went wrong…'

The Romans had suddenly thrown a volley of spears at the chariots in the centre of the attack, and they had crashed into each other, throwing the whole host into confusion. Then the Romans had marched forward like a huge metal beast, protected by their shields, hacking the tribesmen to pieces.

The warriors had turned and fled in panic. Some of them had been so sure of victory they had brought their families in wagons to watch the battle. But the wagons blocked the way out of the valley, and the host was trapped.

'The Romans slaughtered everyone they caught,' whispered my father, 'most of the men from the village, Dragorix, women and children. I was lucky to escape. They say Boudicca and her daughters took poison…'

My father is sleeping now, and Mother is soothing Bryn, who has been crying. I am trying to go to sleep too, but there is a shadow in my heart.

For I know that the Romans are coming, and it is their turn for revenge.

# Chapter 4
# The Coming of Suetonius

*Autumn,* AD *60.*

These are dark times for the Tribe of the
Horse People – rebels caught and crucified,
burned villages and fields, empty bellies.
The Romans swooped on the lands of the
Iceni – and the other tribes who rebelled –
like the Furies.

But, strangely enough, they left our village alone. We waited as the days grew shorter and the nights grew colder, and still the Romans did not come.

Then yesterday, just as the sun was rising, I heard the thud of steel-shod sandals, the clink of sword belts, the harsh barking of the Latin tongue.

We stood in the doorway of our round house, my family and I. My father leaned against the doorpost, his leg better, but painful all the same, Mother holding Bryn, his eyes shining with a baby's wonder at the sight before us.

The village was full of Roman soldiers, the morning sun glinting on their shields and breastplates, their helmet crests and cloaks.

Their faces were hard, and their hands were on their sword hilts. I felt my mother and father put their arms around me, and hold on to each other, too.

A Roman was coming towards us, a Roman in rich armour on a tall horse, a Roman with a crest nodding on his helmet. He reined in the horse and stared down at us, his cold, dark eyes boring into me...

He spoke, but it was in the Latin tongue, and I didn't understand.

'This is Suetonius Paulinus, the governor,' said a nearby Roman soldier, speaking our tongue perfectly, but with a Gaulish accent. 'He's asking if you're the girl who stood up to Boudicca. Goodness knows why he's interested.'

'I am,' I said, and looked Suetonius in the eyes. 'And are you the Roman butcher who burns our villages and our fields and murders my people?'

I heard the fear in my mother's sharp intake of breath, felt my father tense beside me. The Gaulish soldier translated… but Suetonius simply smiled.

'I see now the tale was true,' he said,
and suddenly he drew his sword from the
scabbard, metal hissing on metal. He raised
it high, kissed the hilt. 'I salute your brave
heart, child of the Iceni,' said Suetonius.
'And I give you and your family and
everyone in your village their lives because
of it.'

Then he wheeled his horse round and cantered out of our village, the sun flashing on his sword. And the Roman soldiers followed him, the steady tramp of their marching feet fading as they went down the old trackway. Mother and Father went inside, but I took Bryn and stayed in the doorway...

So that is my story, the tale of how I met Boudicca and Suetonius, and the whole world changed in a year. We are lucky to have our lives, and we know our future on this island – especially mine and Bryn's – belongs to Rome.

But I am Tara Little Flame, I am
thirteen summers old, and I am proud to
be a daughter of the Iceni. And I still have
my brave heart, and I am not afraid.

Whatever the future might hold.

# Glossary

**besiege**  to surround a fortified place, like a castle or a city, and try to make the defenders give up, either by attacking or by starving them out

**Brigantes**  a Celtic tribe who lived in the north of England

**Camulodunum**  Roman name for Colchester

**Cantiaci**  a Celtic tribe who lived in Kent

**Catuvellauni**  a Celtic tribe who lived in Hertfordshire, Bedfordshire and Essex

**Celts**  The Celts came to Britain from Europe over the centuries before the Romans arrived. In Britain they were divided into many tribes. Each tribe had its own territory, and they often fought each other

**chieftain**  the leader of a small clan or village, part of a larger tribe

**Furies**  legendary female demons who pursued wrongdoers and tore them to pieces

**Gaulish**  Gaul was the Roman name for the part of Europe we now call France. It too was mostly inhabited by Celtic tribes who had been conquered by Julius Caesar. They spoke with a Gaulish accent

**Iceni**  a Celtic tribe who lived in Norfolk

**Latin**  the language of the Romans

**legion**  the Roman army was divided into legions, each of which contained 4,000-6,000 men, or legionaries

**Lindum**  Roman name for Lincoln

**Londinium**  Roman name for London

**massacre**  the killing of a large number of people

**Mona**  Roman name for the island of Anglesey, off the coast of North Wales, a specially sacred place in the Celtic religion

**Parisi**  a Celtic tribe who lived along the east coast of Britain and in Yorkshire

**priest**  a person who acts as an official of a religion. Celtic priests were sometimes called druids, and were very important members of their communities

**sacrifice**  killing an animal or a person as an offering to the gods

**standard**  each Roman legion had a standard, a pole with a figure of an eagle on it, and probably the legion's number (the 9th, the 14th and the 20th were in Britain and fought against Boudicca). The standard was carried into battle ahead of the legion

**torc**  a decorated gold neck ring

**Trinovantes**  a Celtic tribe who lived in Suffolk

**Verulamium**  Roman name for St Albans